THE LONELY LION

JOHN GRANT

THE LONELY LION

Illustrated by Susie Poole

HODDER AND STOUGHTON
LONDON SYDNEY AUCKLAND

For Lucy and Hannah.
J.G.

British Library Cataloguing in Publication Data

A catalogue record for this book is available
from the British Library

ISBN 0 340 56883 6 (hbk)
ISBN 0 340 58154 9 (pbk)

First published 1992

Published by Hodder and Stoughton Children's Books,
a division of Hodder and Stoughton Ltd,
Mill Road, Dunton Green, Sevenoaks, Kent TN13 2YA

Printed in Great Britain by Cambus Litho, East Kilbride

Zak lived in a very old house. Some people said that it was haunted! Certainly there were some very strange sounds to be heard from time to time, particularly at night.

Sometimes it was the wind in the chimneys. Sometimes it was owls perched hooting on the roof. Sometimes the noises made Zak's hair stand on end, and he didn't like to think what those were!

One night Zak was wakened by a very mysterious noise. It wasn't the wind. It wasn't . . . well, it didn't make his hair stand on end. And it didn't come from the roof or the chimneys.

It came from the garden!

Zak got out of bed and slipped on his
dressing-gown. He opened the window
and looked down into the moonlit garden.
Two huge yellow eyes looked straight
back up at him.

Zak banged the window shut and
shook with fright.

The noise came again. Someone - or
something - was crying!

Plucking up his courage, Zak opened the window again. Looking up, and sobbing as though its heart would break, was an enormous lion. Tears rolled down its nose, and it wiped them away with a paw the size of a soup plate.

'Please, can I come in?' said the lion in a sniffly voice. 'I'm lost and cold.'

Zak went downstairs and very nervously opened the front door.

'C-c-come in,' he said, 'if you are lost and cold.'

'I'm hungry, too,' said the lion, with a look at Zak that made him more nervous than ever.

'I'm not sure that I have any lion food,' said Zak.

'A slice of toast and a cup of tea will do nicely,' said the lion.

It followed Zak into the kitchen where he put some wood on the fire, and the lion sat down to warm itself while Zak filled the kettle.

'Very nice,' said the lion after a while, brushing toast crumbs from its whiskers. 'You just don't get toast where I've come from.'

'Where's that?' asked Zak. 'Africa?'

'Wigan,' said the lion. 'Wigan Safari
Park. I couldn't stand it a minute longer.
I could have screamed with boredom. I
did one day. Or, at least, I roared.
And . . . there were complaints.'

'Who from?' asked Zak.

'From the visitors because I frightened
them. And from the other lions because I
woke them up. There's nothing to do in a
safari park but eat and sleep.'

'How did you get to *be* in a safari
park?' asked Zak.

'It's a long story,' said the lion. 'I used to perform in Lord Jim's Royal Circus. I had a partner, Bert Ramsbottom. We were Captain Heroic and his Man-Eating Lion. Bert wore his Captain Heroic uniform, and I roared and snarled when he cracked his whip. Then I would leap up on to a little platform and sort of cringe, while the people cheered and clapped Captain Heroic for being so brave. It wasn't easy, I can tell you!'

'What wasn't?' asked Zak.

'Keeping a straight face,' said the lion. 'Trying to look fierce and not to laugh. Because it was all really rather silly. Bert and I were the best of friends. And I do miss him.'

The lion sniffed again and wiped his eyes.

'We always finished the act with Bert putting his head in my mouth. I didn't like that bit. His hairspray tasted awful! And I didn't like it when I had to do silly tricks like walking on my front paws and turning cartwheels. Still, we were a great act, until . . .'

'Until what?' asked Zak.

'A man from the council came one day to see Lord Jim. They didn't like circuses, particularly animal acts. Lord Jim's Royal Circus closed down. I was retired. I don't know what happened to Bert. And I miss him terribly, and the music, and the applause.' And the lion began to cry once more. Then it wiped its eyes and said, 'Now, if you don't mind, I'd like to sleep.' And it curled up in front of the fire and started to snore.

Zak went back to bed and fell asleep wondering what on earth he was going to do with a runaway lion who had been in showbiz!

When he woke in the morning, Zak hoped that perhaps it had all been a dream, but the lion was sitting in the kitchen when he went down.

'How about a spot of breakfast, then?' it said.

They sat down with bowls of cornflakes.

'I rather hoped you might have rice crispies,' said the lion. 'I like listening to them.'

Over toast and coffee, Zak introduced himself.

'Pleased to meet you, Zak,' said the lion. 'I'm called Wallace, after an ancestor of mine. He was famous in his day. He lived in Blackpool Zoo, and they say he ate a boy called Albert. It was never proved.'

Zak switched on the radio. There was a brass band playing.

'That's my music!' cried Wallace.
'"Entry of the Gladiators",' and he leapt
up, knocking over the table and scattering
the breakfast things in all directions.

'I'll show you my act!' he cried.
'Although it won't be the same without
Bert - I mean Captain Heroic.'

'Let's go outside,' said Zak. And he
hurriedly opened the front door before
Wallace did any more damage.

And there, on the lawn in front of
Zak's house, Wallace put on a show.

'Not the same without Bert and the man-eating lion bit,' he explained, 'but I'll show you some of the old silly tricks.' And it was most entertaining all the same as Wallace walked on his back paws, then on his front paws, did somersaults, and turned cartwheels.

As he finished, there was a chorus of chirps, coos, mews, barks and whistles. Four pigeons, a flock of sparrows, two stray cats and the Yorkshire terrier from next door had come to watch.

Wallace bowed low. Then he blew kisses to the audience. 'Thank you! Thank you! Bless you!' he cried, while the tears rolled down his cheeks again.

He's overdoing it a bit, thought Zak, but before he could think any further there was an interruption.

A crowd of men rushed on to the lawn. 'There he is!' they shouted. 'Don't panic! Stay still everybody!'

'What do you mean?' shouted Zak. 'And who are you anyway?'

'It's all right!' they shouted back. 'We know how to deal with dangerous wild animals.'

'Don't be silly!' said Zak. 'It's only Wallace. He's my friend, and my guest. And, what's more, you are trespassing!'

'We are from Wigan Safari Park,' said the man who seemed to be in charge. 'Your friend ran away. He has caused, I may say, considerable inconvenience!'

At that, Wallace started to cry again. His lip trembled as he sobbed, 'Don't let them take me back there! Let me stay!'

'I'd like to,' said Zak. 'But I don't really have accommodation for lions . . . particularly lions who are stars. But I do have an idea. You go back quietly to the safari park and, if my idea works out, everything will end happily.'

So Wallace went with the men to where they had parked their truck. He climbed into the back and the audience waved him goodbye.

Zak hurried into the house. In the phone book he found an entry for the Society of Circus Performers. He spoke to a friendly lady who said, 'Ramsbottom? I don't think –'

'His other name is Captain Heroic,' said Zak.

'Of course,' said the lady, and she gave Zak Bert's address at the Home for Retired Lion Tamers.

Zak wrote a letter:
Dear Mr Ramsbottom,
    You don't know me, but I am
a friend of Wallace the Man-Eating
Lion, and I have a plan . . .
He wrote another letter, this time to
the Manager of Wigan Safari Park.

Meanwhile back at the safari park Wallace was as bored as ever. Until, one day, the manager drove up in his jeep that was painted to look like a zebra. He had a passenger. 'Wallace!' called the manager, 'I have a visitor for you.'

A bald-headed gentleman got down. Wallace looked. No . . . it couldn't be! Yes! It was!

'Bert!' he cried. And the two of them hugged each other while the tears rolled down their cheeks, and the other lions looked on in astonishment. The manager said, 'Mr Albert Ramsbottom is to be the safari park's new lion expert.' Then he drove off again, leaving Bert and Wallace grinning at each other.

Zak paid a visit to Wigan Safari Park. He met Bert, who told him that one of his ancestors had been eaten by a lion at Blackpool so lion-taming was, in a manner of speaking, in his blood.

The two friends are still happily together at Wigan and every year on Zak's birthday, they pay him a visit. There on the lawn in front of the house they put on their act. Bert cracks his whip. Wallace roars and cringes . . . then winks at the audience to show that it is all in fun. And as Bert is bald and doesn't use hairspray Wallace doesn't mind when he puts his head in his mouth. To the great delight of Zak and the pigeons, sparrows, stray cats, and the Yorkshire terrier from next door.

Other titles you may enjoy: